CHARLIE BROWN'S
Christmas Stocking

by

Charles M. Schulz

CONTENTS

Charlie Brown's Christmas Stocking

The Christmas Story

About Charles M. Schulz

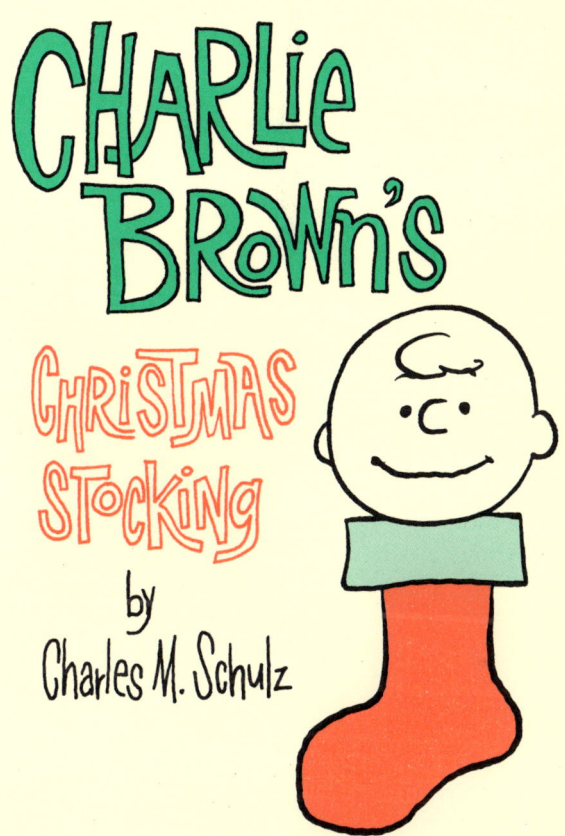

CHARLIE BROWN'S
CHRISTMAS STOCKING

by

Charles M. Schulz

"I'M NOT GOING TO HANG UP A CHRISTMAS STOCKING THIS YEAR... I'VE DECIDED IT'S NOT SCRIPTURAL!"

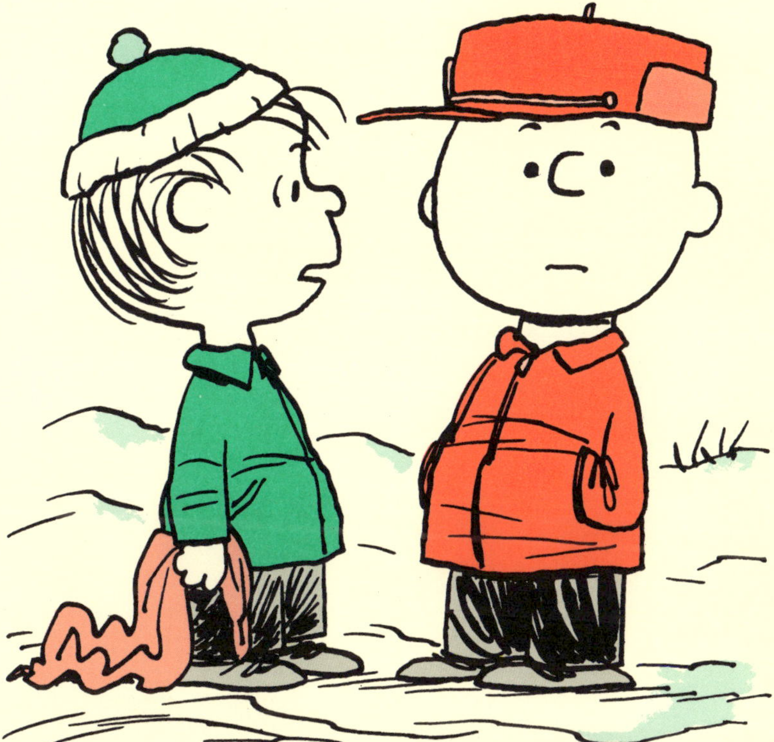

"TWO STOCKINGS?
WHY NOT TWO STOCKINGS?
I HAVE TWO FEET, DON'T I?"

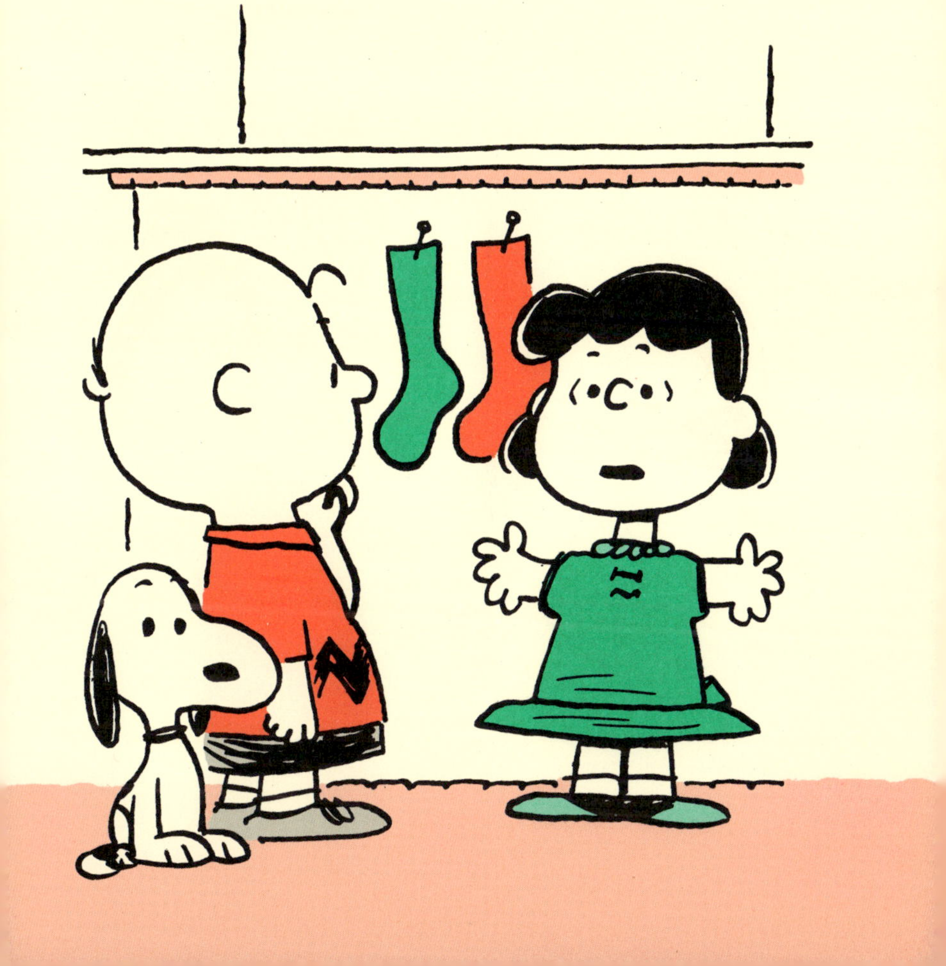

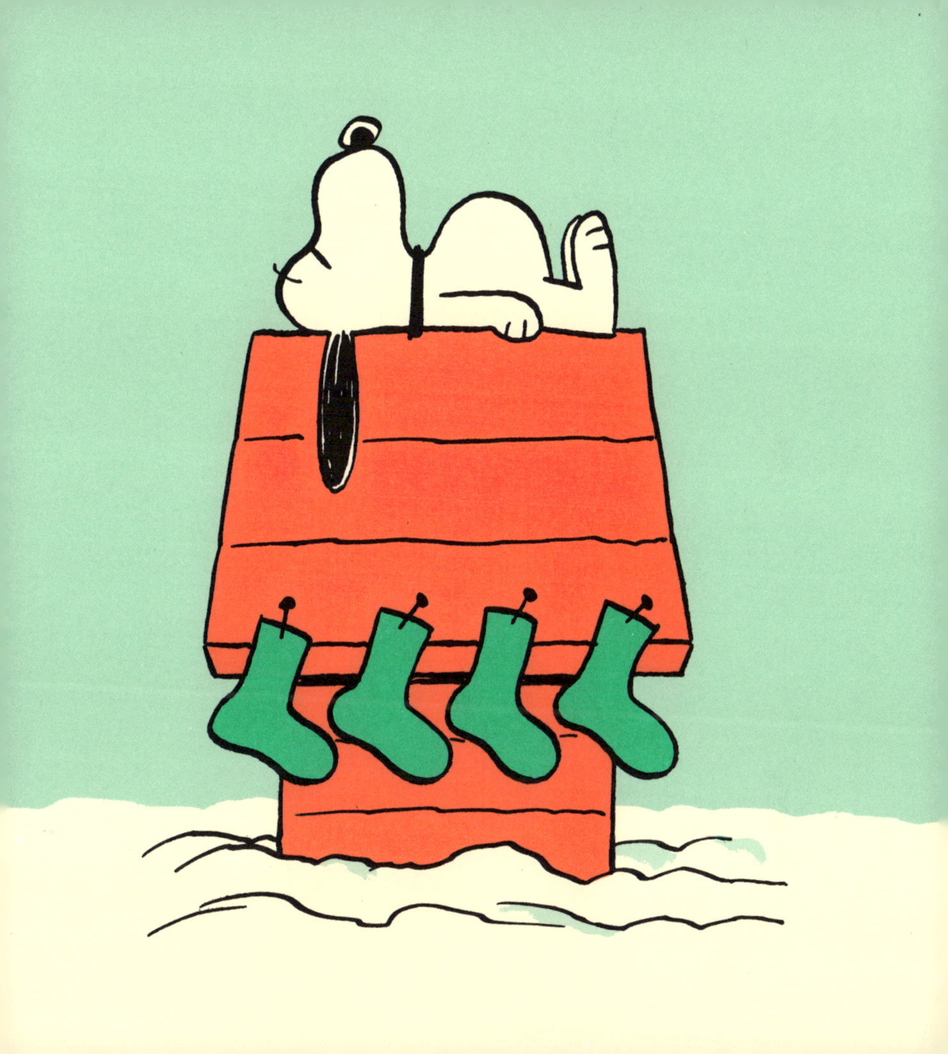

"A CHRISTMAS STOCKING?
I DON'T KNOW IF I WILL OR NOT...
DID BEETHOVEN HANG UP A
CHRISTMAS STOCKING?"

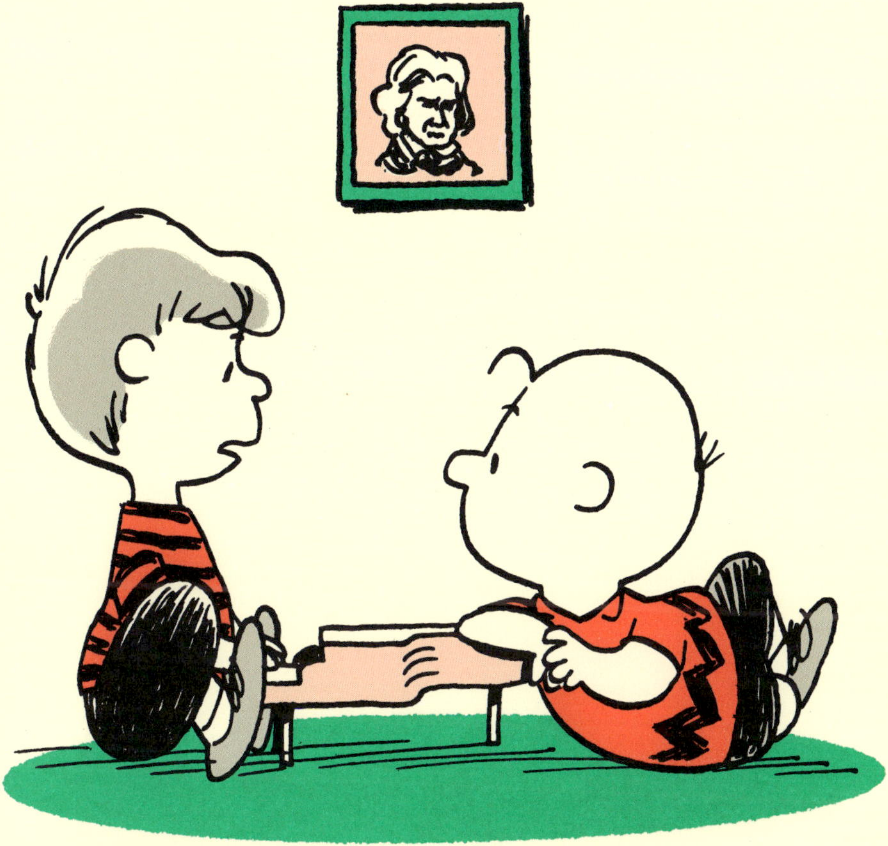

"I'M NOT A BIT WORRIED... THE WAY I SEE IT, HOW CAN SANTA HELP BUT BRING A LOT OF PRESENTS TO A LITTLE GIRL WHO HAS NATURALLY CURLY HAIR?"

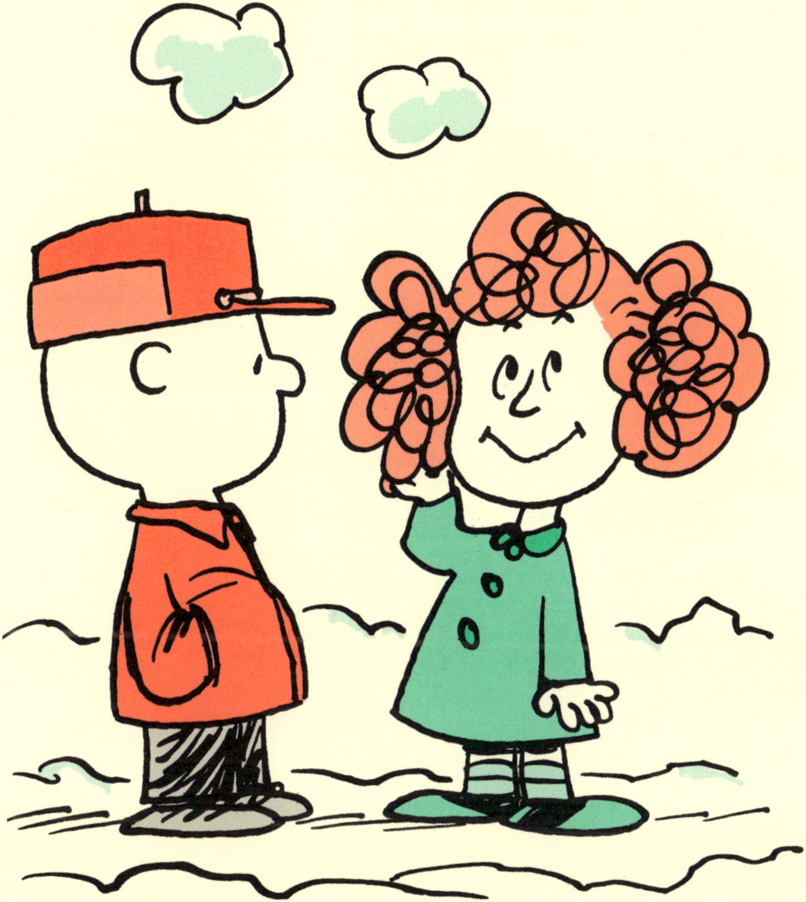

"GROWNUPS ARE THE ONES WHO PUZZLE ME AT CHRISTMASTIME... WHO, BUT A GROWNUP, WOULD RUIN A BEAUTIFUL HOLIDAY SEASON FOR HIMSELF BY SUDDENLY ATTEMPTING TO CORRESPOND WITH FOUR HUNDRED PEOPLE HE DOESN'T SEE ALL YEAR?"

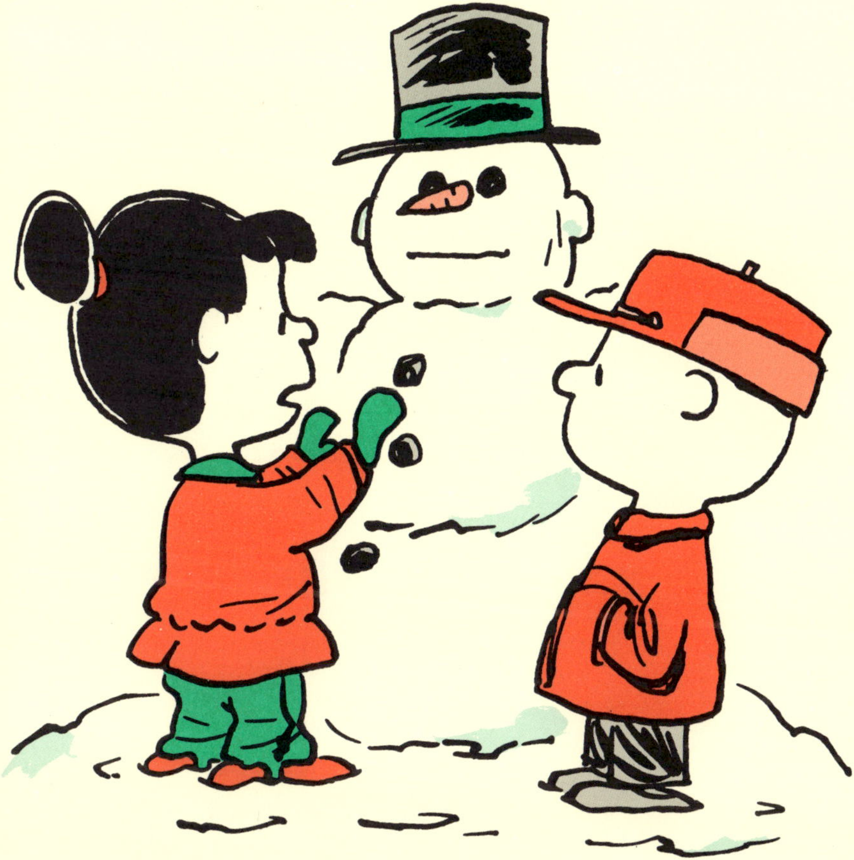

"WHAT WORRIES ME MOST IS HOW SANTA CLAUS IS GOING TO FIND WHERE I LIVE... ON OUR BLOCK, ALL THE HOUSES LOOK ALIKE!"

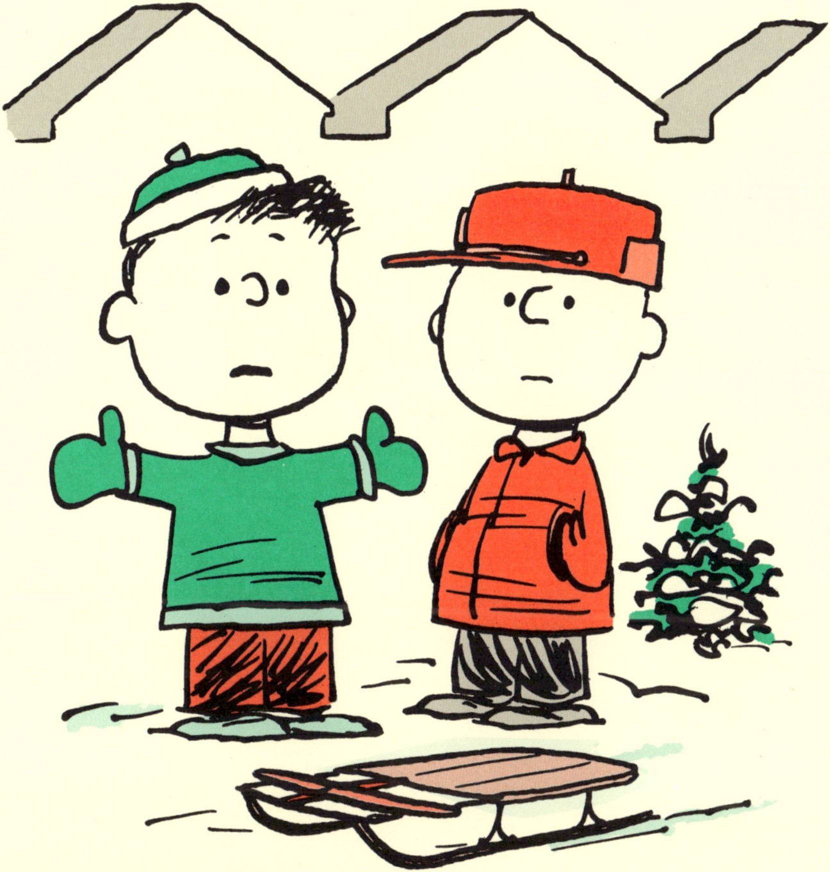

"DO YOU REALIZE THERE'S NO PLACE IN THIS HOUSE TO HANG A CHRISTMAS STOCKING? I SAY LET'S SUE THE ARCHITECT!"

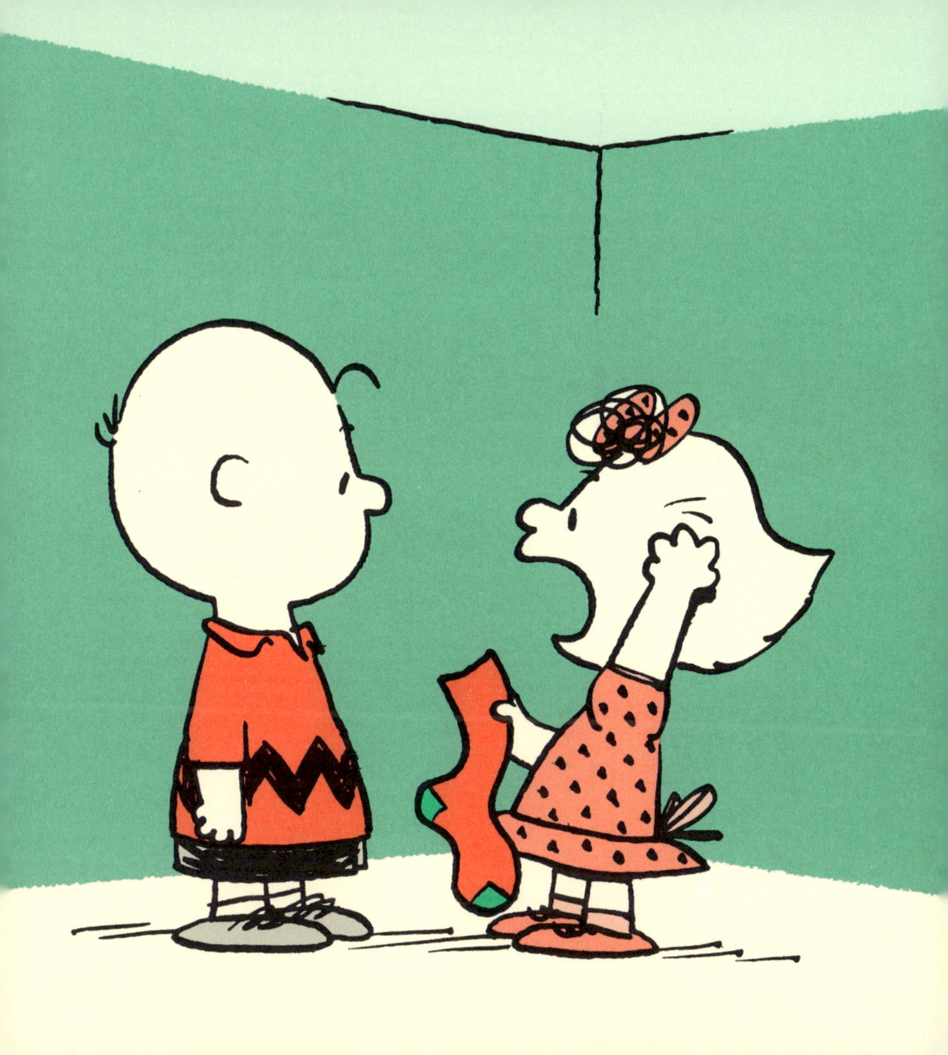

"SHE'S RIGHT...
HOW CAN YOU HANG A CHRISTMAS
STOCKING ON A THERMOSTAT?"

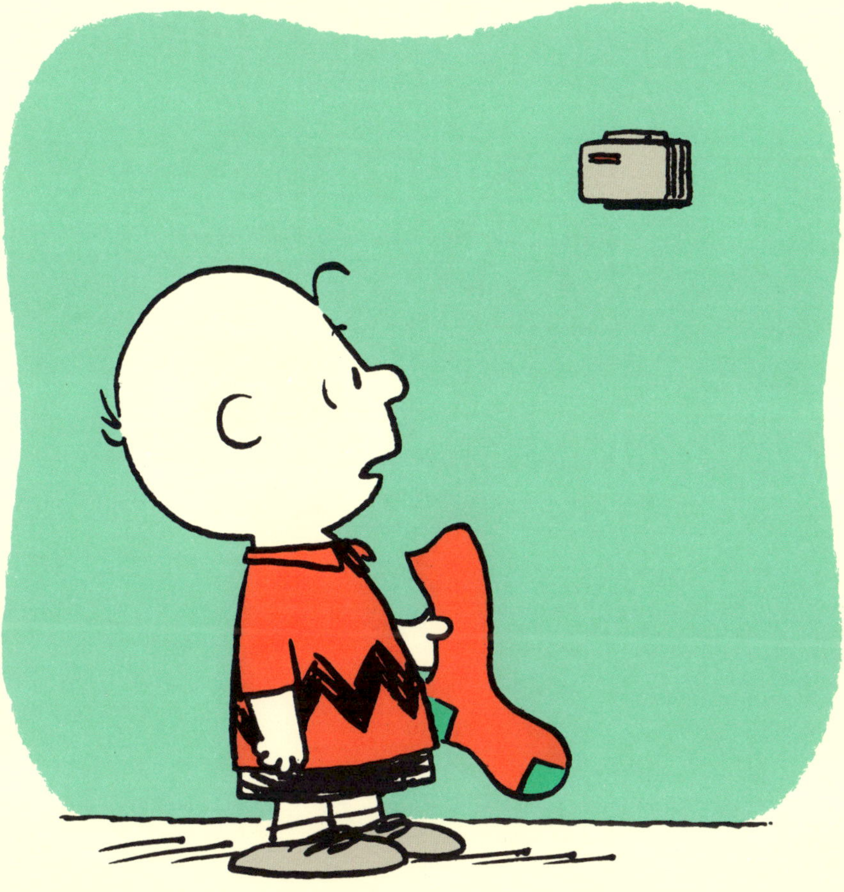

"A HOUSE WITH NO FIREPLACE!
OH, THE TRIALS OF BEING PART OF
THE WRONG GENERATION!"

"SOMEHOW THIS DOESN'T SEEM TO BE THE SOLUTION!"

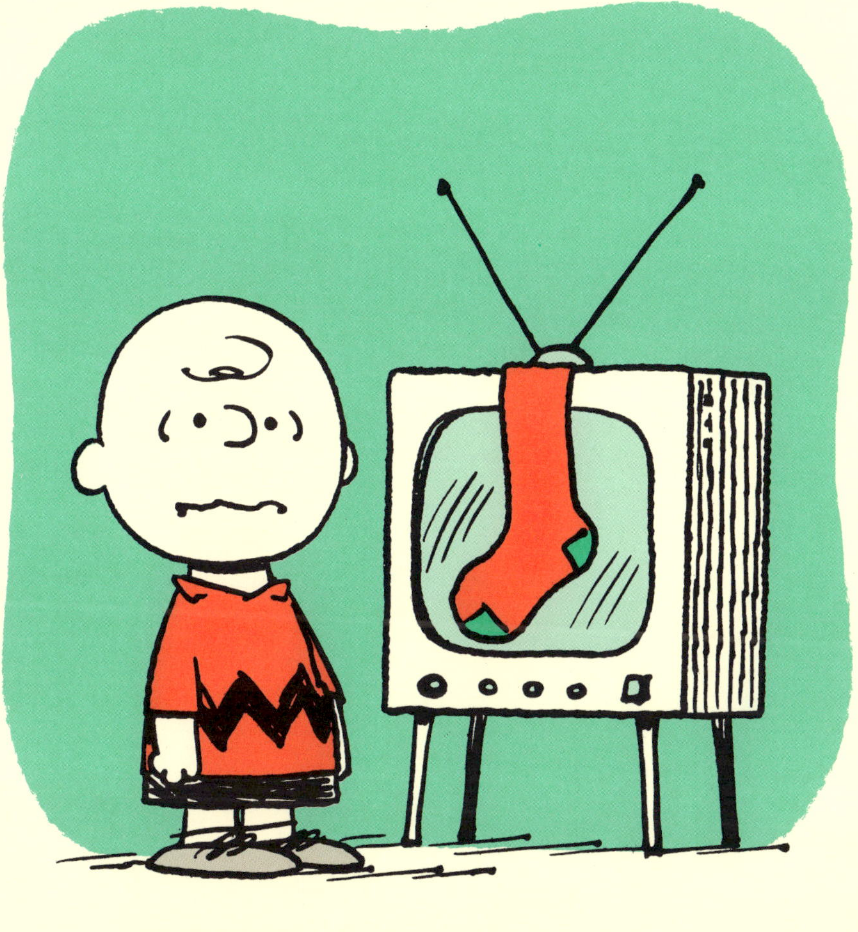

"IT'S ALMOST MIDNIGHT...
GOOD GRIEF!
I FEEL LIKE THE CHAIRMAN
OF THE BOARD DURING AN
INDUSTRIAL CRISIS!"

"THINK OF SOMETHING!
THINK OF SOMETHING!
SANTA CLAUS WILL BE HERE ANY
MINUTE, AND ALL YOU DO IS SAY
YOUR STOMACH HURTS!"

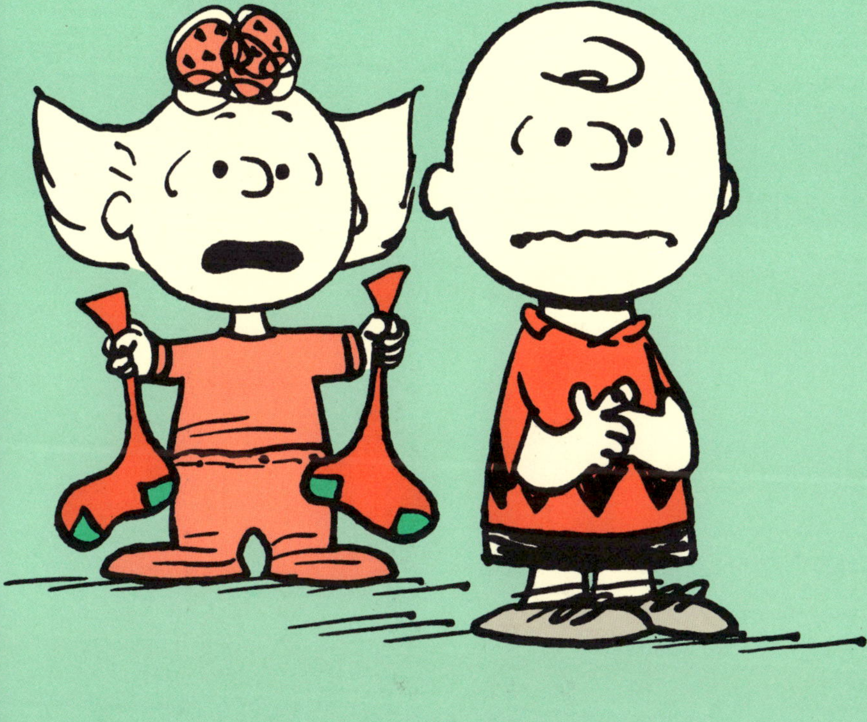

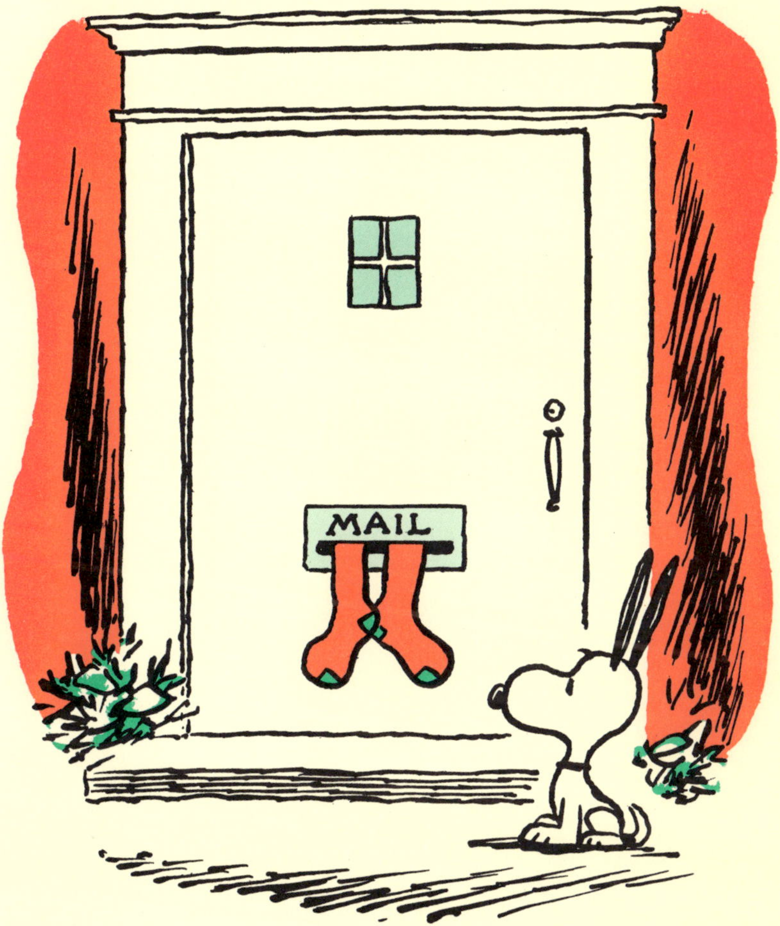
MAIL

"BIG BROTHERS KNOW EVERYTHING...
MERRY CHRISTMAS, CHARLIE BROWN!"

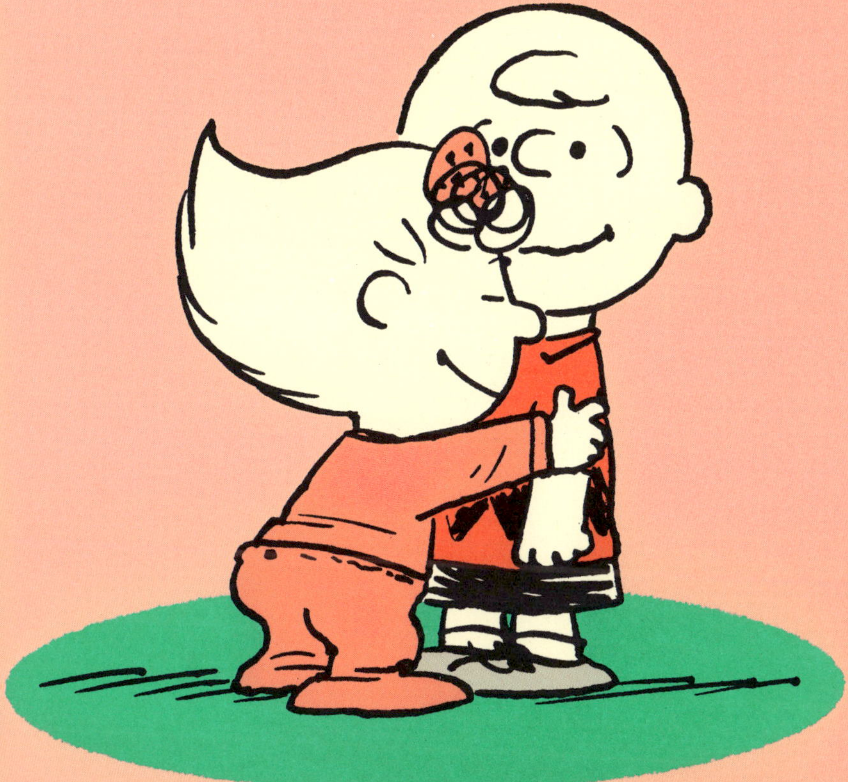

A CHRISTMAS STORY

BY CHARLES M. SCHULZ

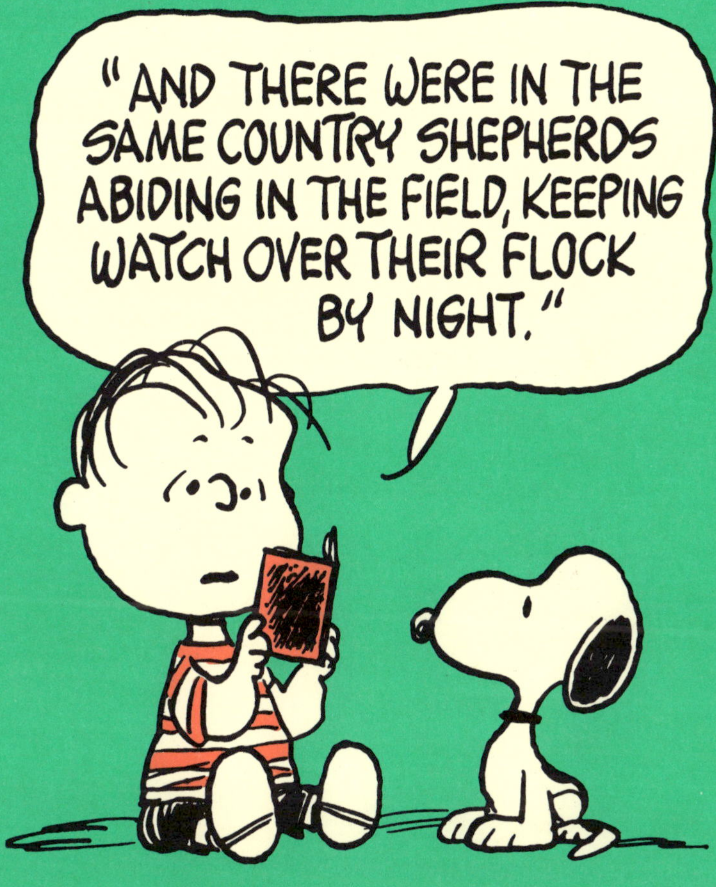
"AND THERE WERE IN THE SAME COUNTRY SHEPHERDS ABIDING IN THE FIELD, KEEPING WATCH OVER THEIR FLOCK BY NIGHT."

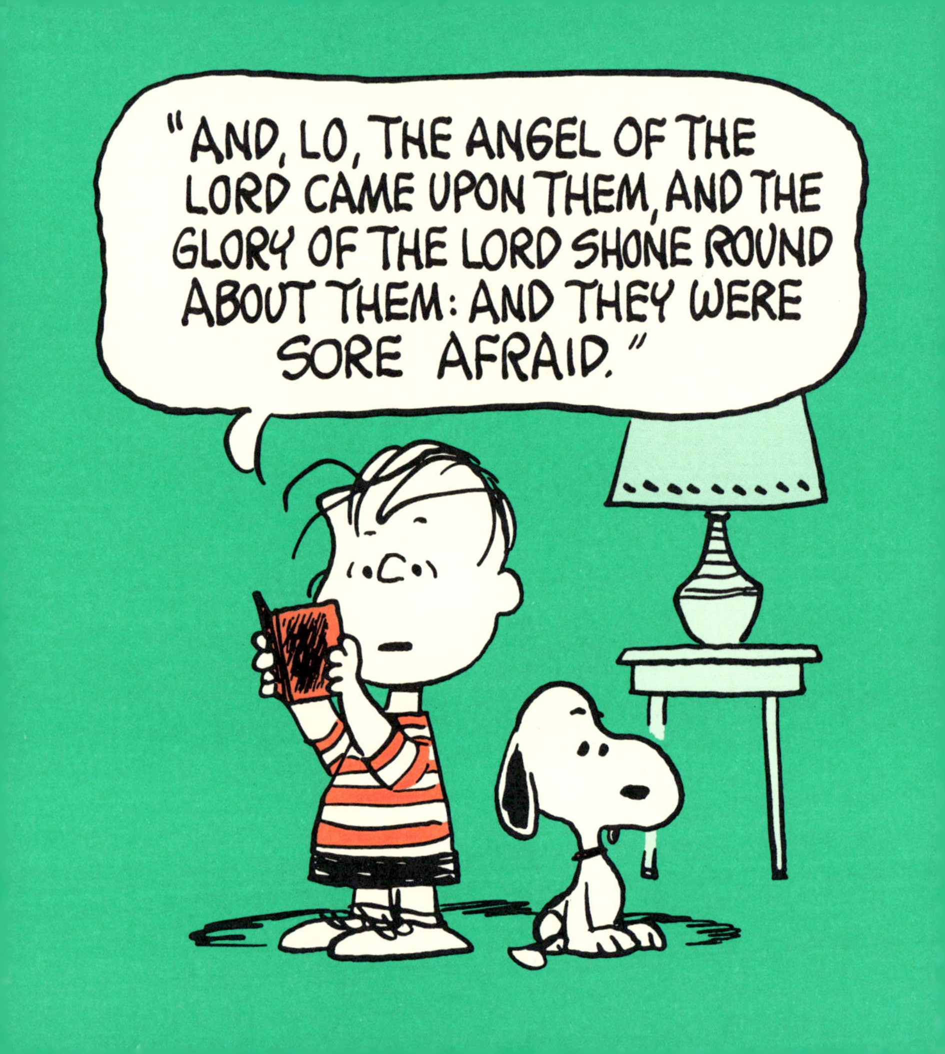
"AND, LO, THE ANGEL OF THE LORD CAME UPON THEM, AND THE GLORY OF THE LORD SHONE ROUND ABOUT THEM: AND THEY WERE SORE AFRAID."

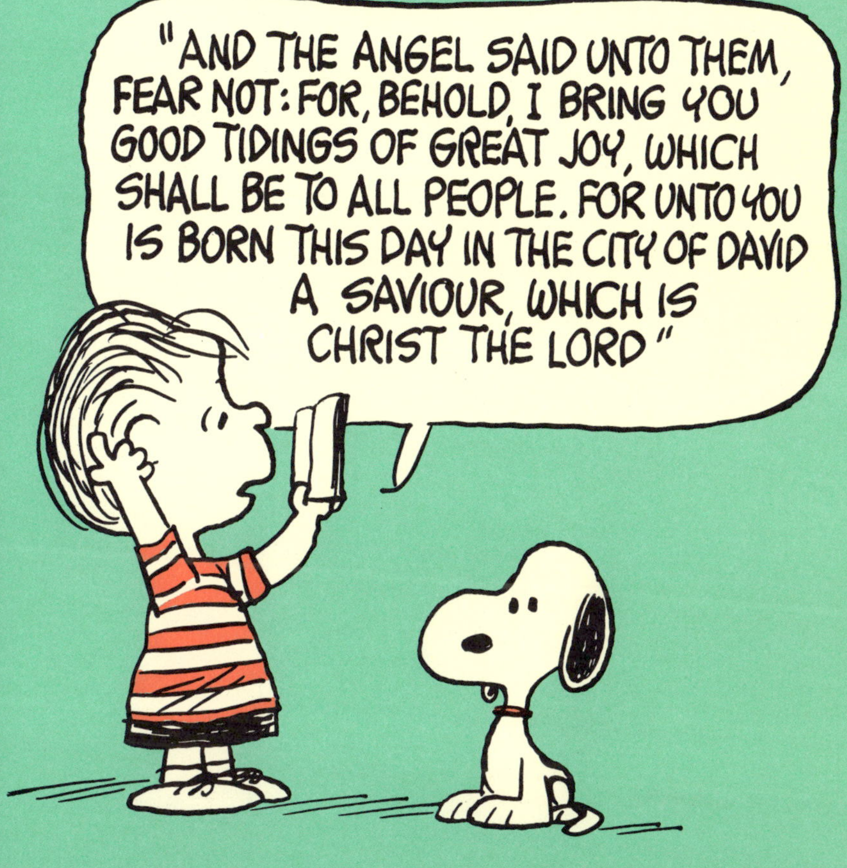
"AND THE ANGEL SAID UNTO THEM, FEAR NOT: FOR, BEHOLD, I BRING YOU GOOD TIDINGS OF GREAT JOY, WHICH SHALL BE TO ALL PEOPLE. FOR UNTO YOU IS BORN THIS DAY IN THE CITY OF DAVID A SAVIOUR, WHICH IS CHRIST THE LORD"

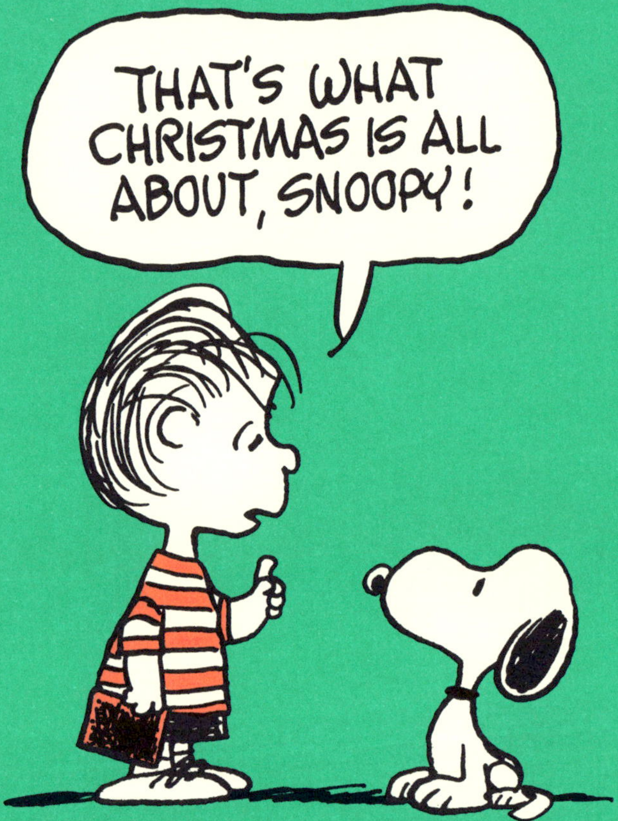
THAT'S WHAT CHRISTMAS IS ALL ABOUT, SNOOPY!

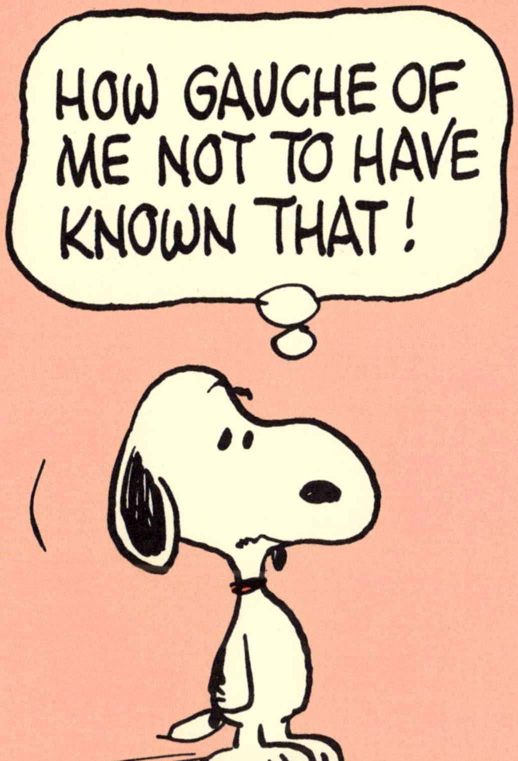
HOW GAUCHE OF ME NOT TO HAVE KNOWN THAT!

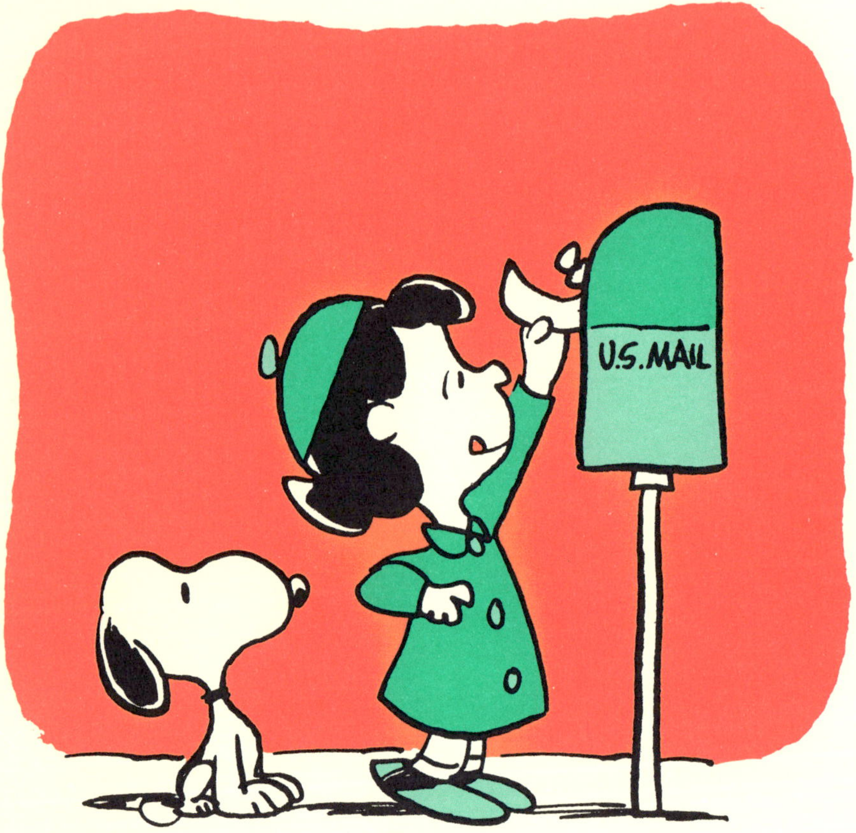
U.S. MAIL

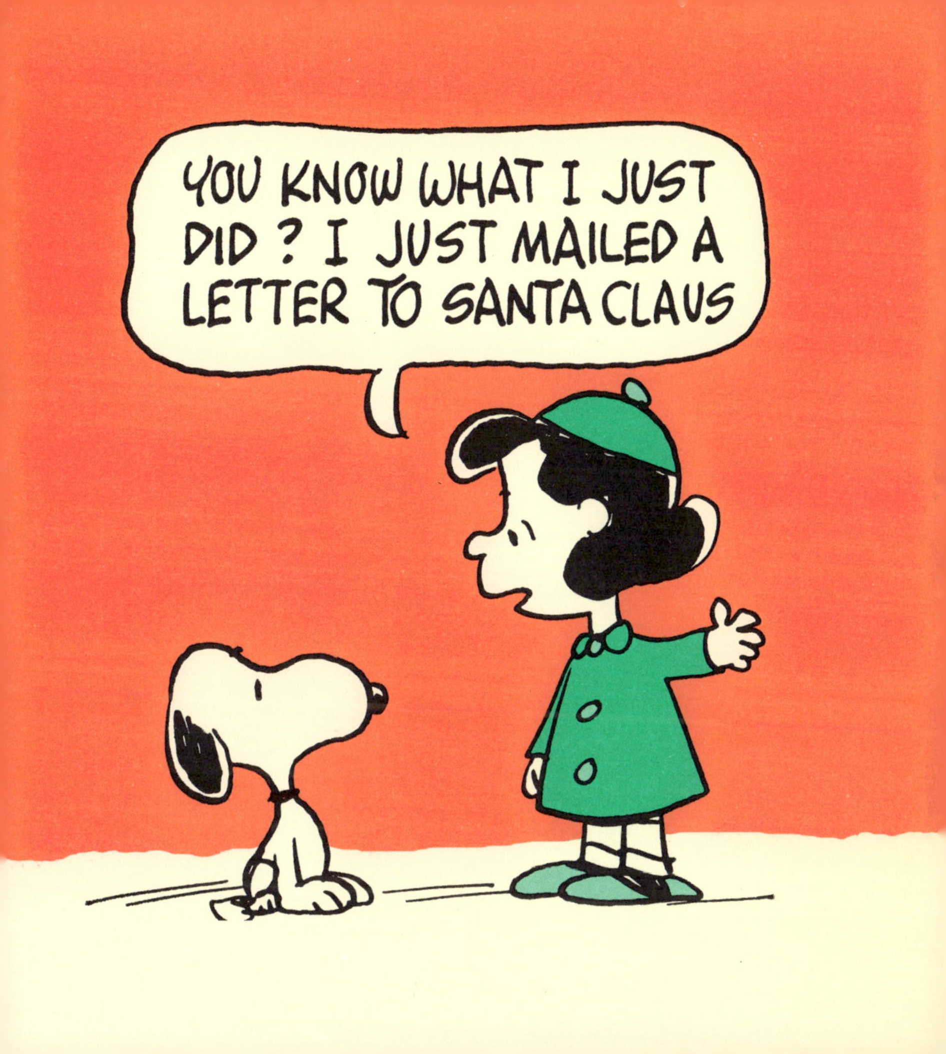
YOU KNOW WHAT I JUST DID ? I JUST MAILED A LETTER TO SANTA CLAUS

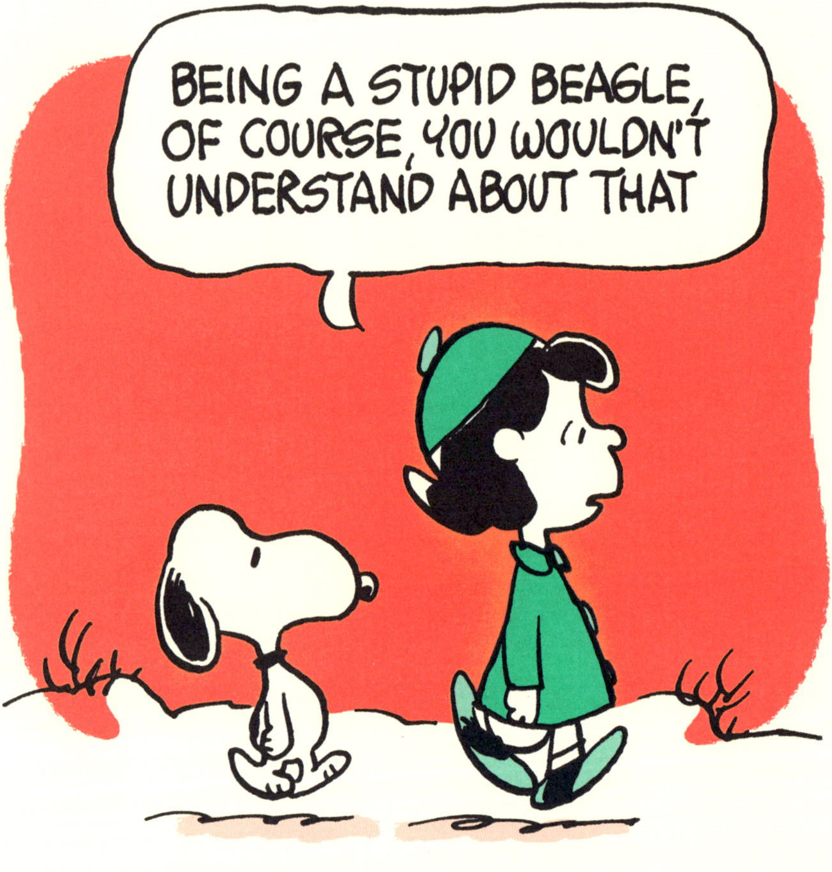
BEING A STUPID BEAGLE, OF COURSE, YOU WOULDN'T UNDERSTAND ABOUT THAT

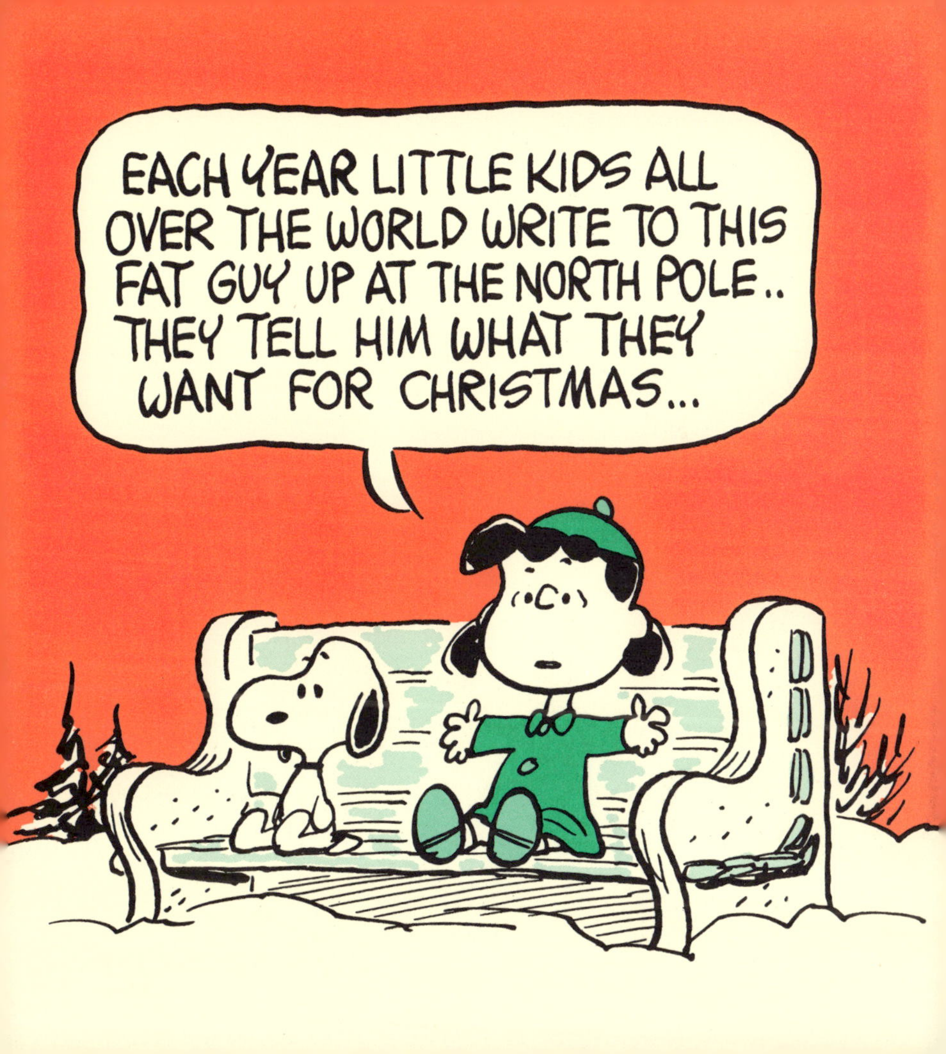
EACH YEAR LITTLE KIDS ALL OVER THE WORLD WRITE TO THIS FAT GUY UP AT THE NORTH POLE.. THEY TELL HIM WHAT THEY WANT FOR CHRISTMAS...

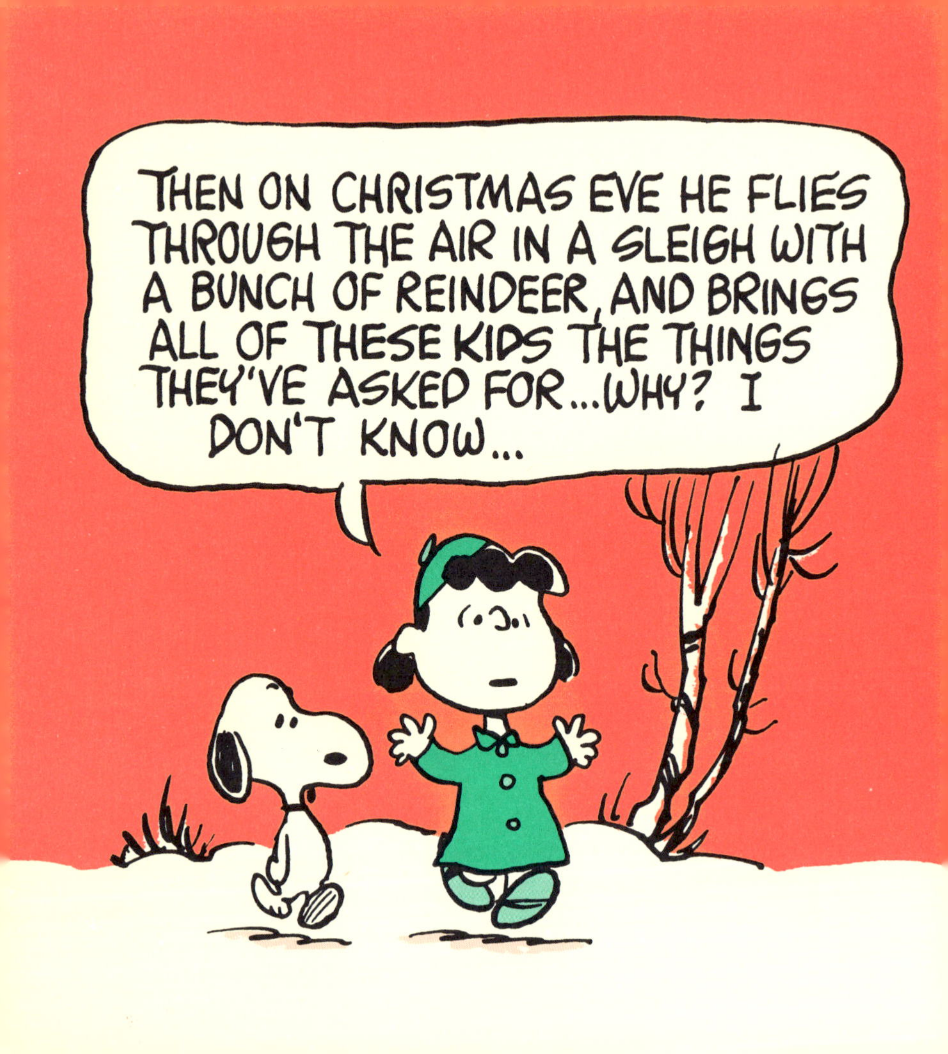
THEN ON CHRISTMAS EVE HE FLIES THROUGH THE AIR IN A SLEIGH WITH A BUNCH OF REINDEER, AND BRINGS ALL OF THESE KIDS THE THINGS THEY'VE ASKED FOR...WHY? I DON'T KNOW...

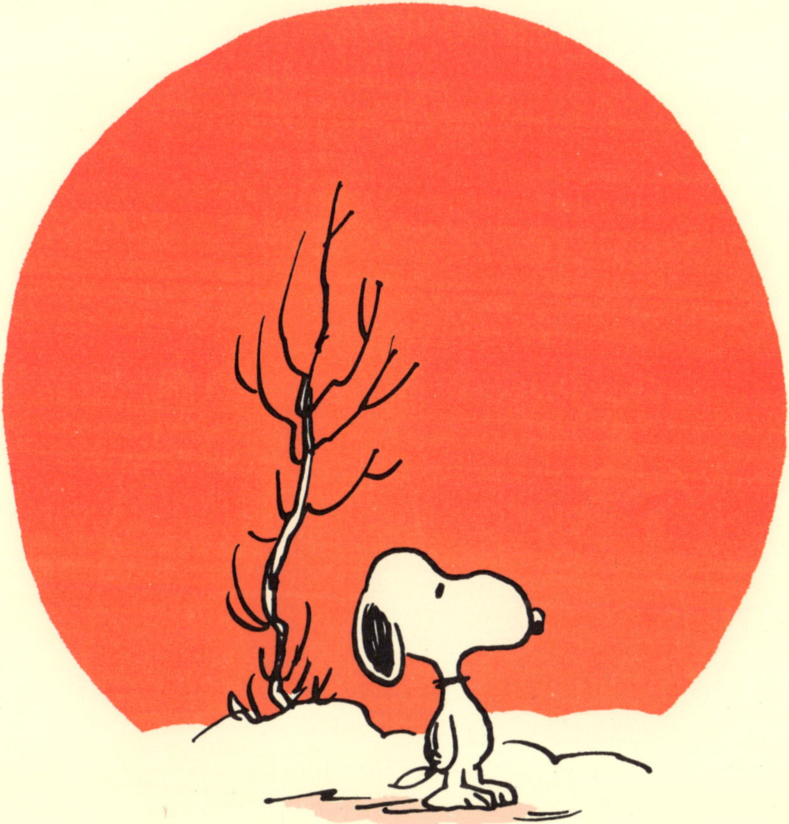

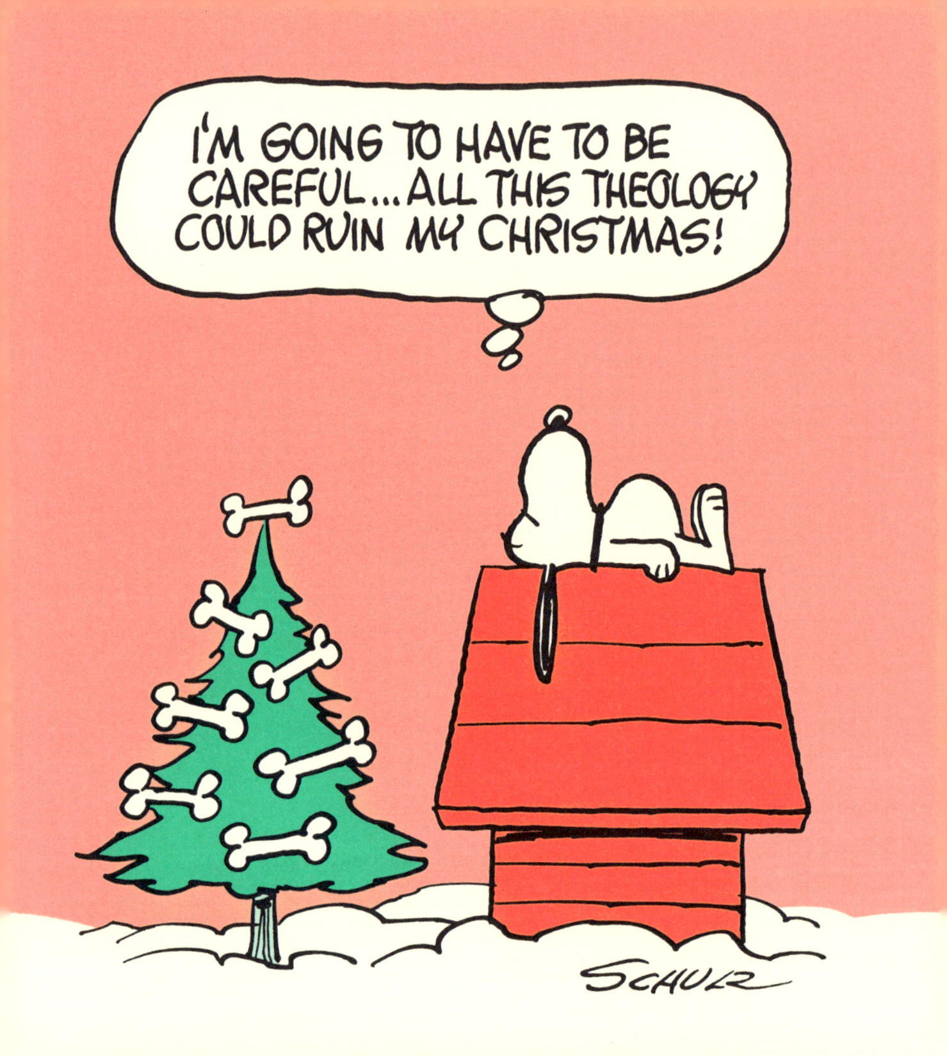
I'M GOING TO HAVE TO BE CAREFUL... ALL THIS THEOLOGY COULD RUIN MY CHRISTMAS!
SCHULZ

Collection conceived and prepared by
Nat Gertler of About Comics
Design: Jacob Covey
VP / Associate Publisher: Eric Reynolds
President / Publisher: Gary Groth

Fantagraphics Books, 7563 Lake City Way, Seattle, WA 98115, USA.
Our books may be viewed on our website at www.fantagraphics.com.

ISBN: 978-1-60699-624-9
Library of Congress Control Number: 2015942838
Third printing: Sepember 2024
Printed in China

About "Charlie Brown's Christmas Stocking"

When "Charlie Brown's Christmas Stocking" first appeared as a little booklet bound into the December, 1963 issue of *Good Housekeeping*, it was ahead of its time. The Peanuts characters were not yet linked to Christmas in people's minds. After all, the Peanuts book *Christmas is Together-Time* wouldn't come out until the following year. More importantly, the TV special *A Charlie Brown Christmas* wouldn't air for two years.

However, the Peanuts gift book *Happiness is a Warm Puppy* had come out the previous year, and spent more than 40 weeks on the best-seller lists, so it was understandable that *Good Housekeeping* wanted to bring some of that Peanuts magic, declaring it their gift to the "12 million women" (and their husbands and children) who read their magazine.

Violet's discussion of grownups "suddenly attempting to correspond with four hundred people" is something that Schulz obviously understood. He and his first wife, Joyce, sent copies of "Charlie Brown's Christmas Stocking" as their own Christmas card to friends.

About "The Christmas Story"

By the time that "The Christmas Story" was the cover feature in the December, 1968 issue of *Woman's Day* magazine, *A Charlie Brown Christmas* was about to air for its third year. With that animated TV special having launched to high ratings and instant acclaim, the Peanuts crew was now associated with Christmas in many people's minds. While the network had been concerned about the religious and biblical content, it proved to be part of the charm of the show. As such, it's not surprising that Schulz opens this piece with Linus reading the Christmas story from the Gospel of Luke, the same material that had been a highlight of the TV special.

Women's Day ran this story across four full-size pages, enlarging some panels and reducing others. For this edition, the story's first appearance in print in over 40 years, the art has been restored to a more consistant size.

About the Author

Charles Monroe Schulz was born in Minnesota in November of 1922. It was only days later that he earned himself the nickname "Sparky," after Sparkplug, a horse in the comic strip Barney Google. And so comics filled his life from the very beginning.

In grade school, he would decorate his classmates' notebooks with popular cartoon characters. He first landed on the newspaper comics page in 1937, when his drawing of the family dog was included in "Ripley's Believe It or Not!"

A correspondence course taught him to be a better artist, and serving in the Army in World War II built his confidence. He became an instructor at the same correspondence school he had once learned from.

Schulz joined the ranks of cartooning professionals in 1947, creating single panel cartoons for the Catholic comic book *Topix* and for local newspapers. These newspaper cartoons were all about kids. When Schulz approached a syndicate about taking the newspaper "Li'l Folks" series national, they convinced him to switch to a multi-panel strip and saddled it with a new name, and thus "Peanuts" was born.

The new strip launched in a handful of papers in the fall of 1950.

By 1952, the first Peanuts strip collection was available in bookstores. The feature grew quickly in popularity and respect, landing Schulz the National Cartoonist Society's Reuben Award for the first time in 1955.

Schulz tried to expand his cartooning base, creating a series of single-panel cartoons about teenagers for the Church of God's Youth magazine from 1955 into the 1960s, and offering up a second newspaper feature, single-panel cartoons about recreational activities entitled "It's Only a Game", from 1957 through 1959. But the 1960s made it clear that "Peanuts" would be his life work as the series jumped from being merely a popular strip to being a pop cultural phenomenon. In 1962 *Happiness is a Warm Puppy,* a book of original Peanuts material, landed on the national best-seller lists and stayed there for most of a year.

1965 brought "A Charlie Brown Christmas," the first full-length Peanuts cartoon. The Peanuts characters landed on stage in 1967's *You're a Good Man, Charlie Brown*. The decade closed with the December 1969 release of the first Peanuts movie, *A Boy Named Charlie Brown*.

Schulz crafted the strip all by himself for almost fifty years. Failing health caused him to announce his retirement from that effort in late 1999, allowing the strip to go into reruns rather than putting it in other hands. He passed away in February 2000, on the same weekend that the final original strip was in the papers.

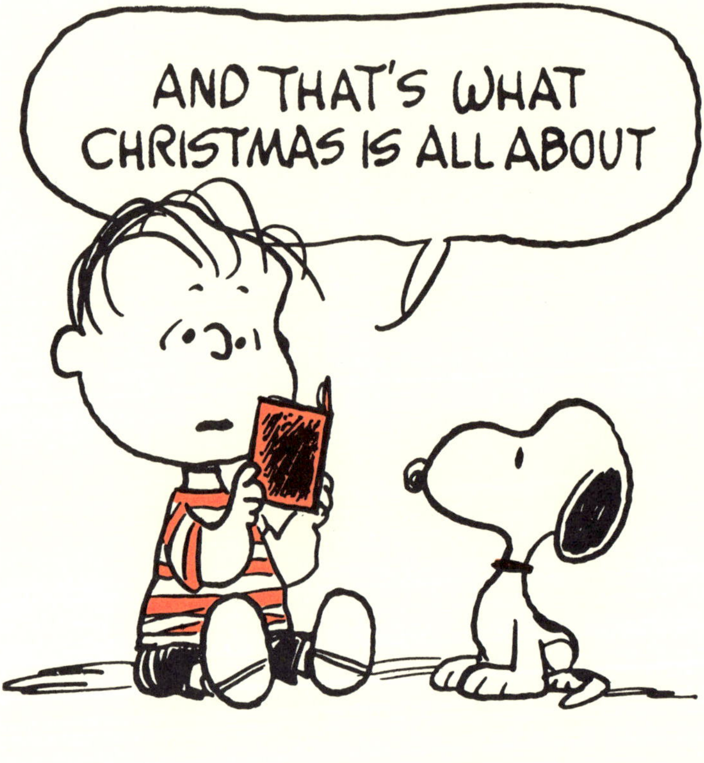
AND THAT'S WHAT CHRISTMAS IS ALL ABOUT